Mrs Morris
Changes Lanes

DEBBIE YOUNG

MRS MORRIS CHANGES LANES

by Debbie Young

© Debbie Young 2021

Published by Hawkesbury Press 2021

Hawkesbury Upton, Gloucestershire, England

ISBN 978-1-911223-81-8 (paperback)
ISBN 978-1-911223-82-5 (ebook)

To Elizabeth, Jane & Susanne

"Regret is a sterile emotion."

**Professor Sir Joseph Rotblat,
Nobel Peace Prize Laureate 1995**

"Why does no-one ever use my proper name these days?"

Juliet Morris

Also by Debbie Young

Sophie Sayers Village Mysteries *(Novels)*

Best Murder in Show
Trick or Murder?
Murder in the Manger
Murder by the Book
Springtime for Murder
Murder Your Darlings
Murder Lost and Found

St Bride's School Stories for Grown-ups *(Novels)*

Secrets at St Bride's
Stranger at St Bride's

Tales from Wendlebury Barrow *(Novellas)*

The Natter of Knitters
The Clutch of Eggs

Short Story Collections

Marry in Haste – 15 Stories of Dating, Love and Marriage
Quick Change – Tiny Tales of Transformation
Stocking Fillers – 12 Short Stories for Christmas

Essay Collections

All Part of the Charm – A Memoir of Modern Village Life
Still Charmed
Young By Name – Whimsical Columns from the Tetbury Advertiser
Still Young By Name

Mrs Morris Changes Lanes

A Second Chance Novella

DEBBIE YOUNG

HAWKESBURY
— PRESS —

1 Jools

"But it's my day off. My only me-time all week."

Juliet glared at the single key her husband Rob had dropped onto the kitchen table beside her bowl of ChocoPops. It wasn't the master that shared a fob with the keys to their front door, his mum's house, and the lock-up from which he ran his plastering business. That fob also boasted a miniature personalised licence plate, ROB 999, a gift from their kids years before.

Not that Rob's car bore a personalised licence plate, and it likely never would, but now and again, getting his round in at the pub, he would casually drop the key fob on the bar, as if offering the barmaid a passport to ride in a fancy sports car. The only personal touch Rob had acquired for his succession of tatty vehicles was a collection of dents, inflicted by pesky drivers who failed to get out of his way or who thoughtlessly parked too close to where he wanted to manoeuvre. He claimed he was just a magnet for bad drivers, but Juliet had long ago accepted he took no greater care of his car than he did of her.

Whenever this solitary key came out of the kitchen junk drawer, Juliet knew it meant he'd booked the car into Dave's Magic Motor Repairs, just off the Cirencester ring road. This only ever happened when the car had become illegal or unsafe to drive. Tied on to the key with a grubby piece of string was a battered cardboard luggage tag, on which Dave had written his real licence plate number in thick marker pen to make it easy to spot on the pegboard in his office.

"Oh, go on, Jools, it won't take you long," he said. Somehow, it always fell to Juliet to drop the car off for repairs and pick it up again. She collected the used cereal bowl he had left on top of the dishwasher and placed it inside the machine. "Besides, what else have you got planned today? You'll probably just have your nose stuck in a library book all day as usual."

Juliet opened her mouth to disagree but couldn't think what to say. Yes, she would spend some time reading. One of the perks of her part-time job as a counter clerk in the local public library was constant access to books. Just as well she didn't have a job in a bookshop, or she'd spend all her wages without leaving her workplace. But before she allowed herself to escape into a novel today, she had planned to catch up with the laundry, hoover through upstairs and downstairs, and tidy up.

She had expected that when the kids left home, the house would be tidier. Instead, Rob seemed to have become even more slovenly on their departure. She wished he'd done so to stop her missing them so much, but she knew he was neither that thoughtful nor that strategic. Early in their marriage, she had realised it was far less stressful to tidy up after him than to try to change his ways.

"Oh, all right, just this once," said Juliet, knowing it would not be.

"Cheers, Jools."

She handed Rob a flask of tea and the lunchbox she'd packed for him. In the early days of his plastering career, when he still worked cash in hand (he'd assured her that was standard practice in his trade), he'd bought his lunch from takeaways or at the pub. Since that nasty run-in with the tax inspector, packed lunches were one of many economies they'd had to make to cover his tax bill.

Juliet had expected to be more affluent with each passing year of their marriage, especially once the kids left home. Her empty nest and meagre bank balance left her feeling impoverished. Still, it could have been worse. Rob could have been sent to prison for tax evasion. Then where would she be? In a tidier house, that's where. Tidy and peaceful.

As usual, she watched Rob walk down the front garden path and climb into his van without waving goodbye. Then she shut the door and leaned against it, closed her eyes and took a deep breath.

"Goodbye, Rob," she said quietly. "And don't call me Jools."

Today she felt more than usually irritated by his use of the hated nickname, a hangover from their schooldays. While some of her friends' nicknames sounded cute and affectionate, 'Jools' seemed lazy and disrespectful, as if she wasn't worth the extra effort it took to pronounce the final two syllables.

When she'd started going out with Rob, she'd told him she preferred to be called by her full name, and when he'd persisted with Jools, she'd let it go, not wanting to nag – a decision she'd regretted ever since. She couldn't bear his continuing desecration of perhaps the most romantic girl's name in the English language. Her namesake's romance hadn't ended well, either.

Jools to rhyme with fools, she thought, heading for their compact lounge. It's not the sort of name you call the woman you love. She wouldn't have minded so much if he'd pronounced it French style, as in Jules Verne, with a soft J and silent s. In her teens, Jules Verne had been one of her favourite authors, fuelling her dreams of adventure and discovery. The closest she'd ever got to emulating Verne's heroes was 'Around the Ring Road in 80 Minutes'.

Ironically, it had been Rob's car that had first attracted her to him. Or at least, his offer of a lift home on a rainy night after a sixth form disco. As one of the oldest boys in their class, he'd passed his driving test early in the academic year. He had worked in a factory

4

during the previous summer holidays and saved up enough money to buy an ancient Hillman Imp. A ride in an old banger had seemed a better offer than being walked home in the rain by the other boy keen on her, Thomas Jenkinson.

Tom had passed out of her life all too soon. Even before he earned the best set of A Levels in the school, he was a dead cert for university. Juliet had no idea what he'd gone on to study, but assumed he'd be earning a fortune now. What if she'd married him instead of Rob? She should have had the wit to wait for him to finish his education and launch his career, instead of rushing to the altar with Rob. If she hadn't been in such a hurry, she could have been living in luxury now, in a big fancy house, with a cleaning lady to do all the chores, and a husband who truly loved her.

But on life's journey, Tom had taken a different exit from the roundabout, heading for the motorway of academic excellence in distant parts, while Juliet took the earlier turn-off for non-motorway traffic only. Their paths had not crossed since. She'd never even moved away from her hometown and was still employed by the library where she'd worked as a schoolgirl.

As Juliet straightened the sofa cushions and binned three empty crisp packets, she told herself an optimist might count this as me-time. Wasn't it a treat-to-self to make the house nice and tidy? Juliet delved between the side cushions of Rob's armchair to dig out the remotes and return them to the shelf beneath the television.

She would appreciate the more orderly surroundings, even if Rob didn't. Rob wouldn't notice if the corduroy scatter cushions were in the fish tank glugging away on the sideboard, or if the fake sheepskin rug was on top of the coffee table, as long as his view of the television was uninterrupted. Once, catching the end of a psychology documentary while waiting for the football to come on, Rob had told Juliet it wasn't his fault he was so untidy. It was his mother's, for conditioning him. In his formative years, she'd always tidied up after him.

Next on her to-do list was to clean the bathroom and load the washing machine. Not having to look at the overflowing dirty clothes basket would also make her happier. Rob said she was always in a better mood after folding and putting away the laundry.

After a couple of hours of housework, Juliet decided to treat herself to a more self-indulgent reward. At eleven o'clock, she would eat one of her favourite chocolate bars with her morning coffee. Alone in the house with no-one watching, she would dip the chocolate bar in her coffee – a cheaper alternative to buying a mocha from a café – just like the television adverts which present chocolate as the perfect companion for lone women. She brought her cup and saucer from the kitchen into the lounge and set it down on the coffee table, now pleasingly free of used tissues, discarded socks and toenail clippings.

Juliet reached for her knitting bag and unzipped the small side pocket in which she kept her secret stash – a place that Rob, peckish after an evening at the pub, would never think of raiding for snacks. Nor would the kids before they'd left home a few years before.

Using a delicate cup and saucer, the only piece of bone china in the house, also counted as a treat. Jessie had bought it for her from a jumble sale for Mother's Day when she was about ten. Juliet only ever used it when she was alone for fear of anyone else breaking it.

On the days she was at work, morning coffee was taken in one of an assortment of chunky mugs bearing brand names of the library's commercial suppliers. Too often, she ended up with the one promoting the sanitary disposal bins in the ladies' toilets.

Juliet peeled the plastic wrapper from the chocolate bar and dropped it neatly into the wastepaper basket beside the sofa. Slowly, in a practised movement, she dunked the chocolate into her coffee, lowering it almost to the bottom of the cup. At the point of optimal softness, she pulled it back out and raised it to her lips, keeping her cup and saucer beneath her chin to catch any drips, because chocolate stains are hell to shift. Inserting the bar into her mouth, she felt like the Little Crocodile in *Through the Looking Glass*, whose description she'd enjoyed sharing during Junior Story Time the day before.

How cheerfully he seems to grin,
How neatly spreads his claws,
And welcomes little fishes in,
With gently smiling jaws!

She closed her eyes in rapture as her teeth sank into the chocolate at the point of least resistance, the indentation between the first two segments.

Then – crunch! Her jaw rebounded from something more solid than melting chocolate. Juliet winced as hard as Rob had done on his car's most recent encounter with a traffic island.

This made no sense! Even if she'd eaten the chocolate straight from the fridge, it should not have provided that much resistance. Had she inadvertently bought a bar studded with whole hazelnuts? It wouldn't be the first time.

Juliet set the rest of the bar on her saucer as she examined the severed chunk with her tongue. Nope, no nuts – but there was something sharp embedded in the molten mass of chocolate as yet unswallowed. When she spat it out into her teaspoon, a tiny meteorite glinted back at her. Running her tongue over her teeth, she discovered its origin: a jagged upper right tooth. Journey to the Centre of the Cavity.

It didn't seem fair that only that morning, she'd crunched her way through a bowl of bland breakfast cereal without mishap, but had met her tooth's nemesis in a softened bar of her favourite chocolate. Maybe the crunchy cereal had created a fault line. The hole felt like a crater on the moon.

As Juliet gritted her teeth in resignation, a searing pain shot from jaw to temple, making her cry out. When she stopped biting down, the pain didn't recede.

Her appetite for chocolate destroyed, Juliet set her cup and saucer on the coffee table. So much for her me-time. Such agony called for emergency treatment. And no, ending the agony would not count as me-time.

She went into the hall and picked up the phone to call the dentist.

"You'd like an emergency appointment today, Mrs Morris?" The receptionist's tone suggested there was no question she would rather be asked. "Well, it's your lucky day. I've just put the phone down from a cancellation. Can you get here by midday? Good. I'm sure the dentist will be very pleased to see you."

I bet he will, thought Juliet sourly, feeling as if she'd just booked a trip to the confessional. Not that she was Catholic, but visiting the dentist always made her conscious of her sins of omission and commission – not flossing regularly, eating too many sweets.

"Yes, noon would be perfect, thank you," she replied. "I can just fit that in before I take my husband's car to be repaired. My lucky day indeed."

2 Mrs Morris

Juliet had tried not to transfer her fear of dentists to her children. She was relieved that Jessie and Jake had grown up with reasonably intact teeth, at least until they'd left home a few years before, Jessie to work at a fancy hair salon in Bristol and Jake as a plumber in Gloucester. Juliet was glad they were close enough to come home for the occasional weekend, even if they did bring their laundry. Jessie had offered to do Juliet's hair for free at home when she had time, and Juliet was still looking forward to that moment. She liked to think she and Rob could rely on Jake to fix any plumbing issues, should the need arise. They were good kids really.

Juliet's fear of dentists wasn't a rational aversion to pain, but more an embarrassment at exposing her vulnerability. She considered each cavity a personal failure, proof of her poor life choices. Some errors of self-care were reversible. A bad haircut or over-plucked eyebrows would grow back eventually. Which was just as well, given the abuse she and her best friend Maisie had inflicted on their appearance in their teens.

Changes to teeth, however, were less reversible, unless you had the huge disposable income required for private cosmetic surgery. Juliet had to depend on the NHS for her dental care. At least it made treatment affordable.

Just before noon, she entered the premises of her regular high-street dentist. Well, regular for the kids, at least. She'd left it so long between her own last two visits that the dark-haired dentist, Mr Allsop, had in the meantime turned grey. At first, she'd assumed he was a different dentist altogether, and she'd been taken aback when he greeted her as if he knew her. Then she recognised above his mask his distinctive blue eyes. One had an iris larger than the other, like David Bowie's. Sometimes, while he was at work on her mouth, she'd pretended he was David Bowie to take her mind off the drill. David Bowie had naturally wonky English teeth before he succumbed to expensive veneers. She felt as if they were kindred spirits.

After registering at reception, Juliet took a seat in the pale mauve waiting room and watched the neon tropical fish swim up and down their tank. She was glad they had the hardier cold-water type at home, otherwise she might get toothache every time she looked at them. The fish and the tank had been Jessie's fifteenth birthday present. When Jessie moved into her cramped city-centre flat share, she was unable to find space for the tank, nor indeed most of her belongings. Jake's flat was also quite small, so the children's bedrooms were still much as they'd been when they'd left home. The only difference was that Juliet didn't have to tidy them so often, only after their occasional weekend visits. Both kids preferred the minimalist look for their flats, a style Juliet could only fantasise about in the cluttered family home.

A pretty young dental nurse in sugar-pink scrubs appeared in the doorway. The practice's soothing pastel colour scheme made Juliet think of sugared almonds. The other waiting patients looked up eagerly from their magazines and phones. You'd think the nurse was about to announce a winning lottery number, thought Juliet.

"Mrs Morris, please."

Losing number, more like. Clumsy with nerves, she gathered up her coat and bag.

The nurse led Juliet up a pistachio-coloured stairway to the plain white door of the treatment room, chatting to put her at her ease.

"How are you today, Mrs Morris?"

Even after thirty years of marriage, Juliet felt odd being called Mrs Morris, a name she associated with her late mother-in-law. Juliet had never liked calling her Mum. That title belonged to her widowed mother, who had struggled to raise her alone for nearly two decades.

"Fine, thank you," Juliet replied automatically, wondering how the nurse might react if she told her the truth: fed up, put upon and in pain. "Thank you for fitting me in at such short notice."

The nurse opened the door to the treatment room and stood back to allow Juliet to enter first.

"It's a pleasure. Glad we can help. Just pop your things down there, then take a seat in the big chair and the dentist will be with you in a moment."

Juliet deposited her coat, bag and car keys on the side table before lowering herself into the dentist's chair, already in a semi-recumbent position. Just pretend it's a beach recliner, only without the sunshine and cocktails, she told herself. Make the most of this rare chance to sit back and relax.

As she wriggled to make herself comfortable, the squeaking of the cold plastic upholstery was the only sound in the room, apart from the brisk rattle of a computer keyboard beneath the dentist's lean fingers. Perched on a wheeled stool at the counter that ran round three sides of the room, he had his back to Juliet as he called up her records on his screen.

Juliet wondered when Mr Allsop's hair had reverted to its original black. Why such vanity in a successful professional? Immediately, she admonished herself for judging him. She wouldn't have criticised a woman for retaining the hair colour of her youth. In fact, she had been thinking of asking Jessie to colour hers when she finally found time. Her natural chestnut was fading to pale tangerine, diluted by ever more greys.

If only Jake had become a dentist instead of a plumber, he might have rejuvenated her smile, too. Not that her smile had much use these days.

"So, it's Mrs Morris now, is it?" When the dentist spoke, she realised he was not Mr Allsop after all. His voice was deeper, richer, more resonant than her regular dentist's. He was peering at her dental chart with as much interest as if he'd never seen anything like it. She hoped he knew what he was doing. Juliet recalled taking Jake to the local hospital after he'd damaged two toes in a school football game. As the doctor brought up Jake's X-ray on his screen, Juliet had gasped in horror.

"I may not be medically trained," she ventured, "but I think you'll find that's a hand, not a foot."

The doctor had laughed it off.

"Ay, yes, we have quite a few patients on our system named J Morris."

It was bad enough having three of them in her household. She had long regretted naming both her children to echo her own first initial. At first, she'd thought it cute, but soon realised it made her less unique. Throughout their education, every time she saw a school report with "J Morris" on the cover, her stomach had jolted, as if her own performance were under scrutiny. She'd given away her own name.

Now Juliet seized the opportunity to speak before the dentist could fill her mouth with the inevitable surgical instruments. "Yes, Mrs Morris. Juliet Morris. Just in case you have any other Mrs Morrises on your system, ha-ha."

He didn't reply. If this was a new dentist, she was not getting off to a very good start with him. How rude still to have his back to her. Where was Mr Allsop, anyway? Mr Allsop was the only dentist she'd seen for years. That was one reason she came here, because the practice always let you see the same dentist. Familiarity made her fear manageable. Better the dentist you know…

The new dentist snapped on a fresh pair of blue rubber gloves from the box beside his keyboard and stretched his hands, scissoring his fingers to perfect their fit. Only after donning a new surgical mask did he finally turn to face her. Even then, he didn't bother to get up. Instead, he propelled his stool on noiseless castors across the floor, using feet clad in distinctly unclinical midnight-blue suede shoes. He came to a halt at her side, looking pleased with his precise control of his vehicle.

Resigning herself to her fate, Juliet clasped her hands across her stomach, resolving to remain dignified this time. On her previous visit, she'd gripped the arms of the chair, white-knuckled, throughout an extraction. Now she tried to imagine she was lying on a poolside lounger in Mediterranean sunshine. This would have been easier had she ever been to the Med, but the more familiar beach at Weston-super-Mare didn't have the same therapeutic appeal.

What a long time it seemed since her first solo trip as an adult to the dentist, when she was expecting Jake. She'd only gone to take advantage of the NHS's free dental treatment for pregnant women.

"I've heard pregnancy wrecks your teeth," she'd said by way of apology when Mr Allsop detected several new cavities.

"What, you mean unborn babies leach the calcium from their mothers' teeth?" Mr Allsop had snorted with laughter. "That's a popular misconception. It's just that most pregnant ladies like to get everything done while it's free. You wouldn't believe how many pregnant patients tell me they haven't been to the dentist since their schooldays."

"Really?" Juliet forced a laugh, trying to sound disbelieving. She didn't return to Mr Allsop's office until she was expecting Jessie.

Now from her prone position, Juliet squinted down her nose to assess the new dentist. He was taller than Mr Allsop, and his shoulders and chest were broader and stronger. Handy for pinning down recalcitrant patients, she thought, and a more effective distraction than thinking about the seaside. She closed her eyes so as not to stare.

There was something strangely familiar about him, as if she was seeing someone she knew outside of their usual context. She'd often mistaken a young person in the library for a friend of her kids before realising she only knew them from the supermarket checkout. Once, recognising their family GP in the local swimming pool, she'd been repulsed by Dr Parsons's near-naked body with its flabby thighs and bulging tummy. It was like seeing a dentist with false teeth.

"What can we do for you today, Mrs Morris?" the new dentist was asking. The way he said "Mrs Morris" reminded her of the gently sarcastic way that her high-school teachers had addressed cheeky pupils as Miss or Mr plus their surname. Miss Deaves, in Juliet's case, although as one of the quieter ones in her class, she largely went unnoticed by the teachers.

"I lost a filling this morning."

Juliet opened her mouth to show him, stiffening as he leaned in for a better look. As he inserted a metal probe with one hand and a tongue depressor with the other, Juliet couldn't help but observe his deep brown eyes. She'd seen them somewhere before; those neat eyebrows, too, although they were bushier than she remembered. Men's eyebrows did get bushier as they aged. Rob's had, anyway.

Juliet flinched as the dentist inserted the probe into the cavity.

"Sensitive?" he asked gently. "Any pain?"

"No," she replied as well as she could with her mouth full. For it wasn't the probe that had startled her. She'd just realised the last time these eyes like that had been so close to hers, the encounter had ended with a kiss.

Thomas Jenkinson's eyes! It had been over thirty years since she'd last seen him, on A Level results day.

Juliet had been disappointed not to see Tom between their last day at school and that fateful day in August when his place at a distant university had been confirmed by his straight As. He hadn't even hung around to celebrate, his parents whisking him away in their big posh car before she could sneak in a congratulatory hug. Her own results didn't matter. She'd been offered more hours at the library, so that was her career sorted. There was no pay rise, as she had no professional qualifications, but the increase in hours took her to full-time equivalent, so it felt like a win. She may not be going anywhere, but she could sate her wanderlust through the pages of library books.

Ever since, Juliet had berated herself for not pursuing her relationship with Tom before he moved away. Did it even count as a relationship? Gentle flirtation during their last term at school, with stolen glances at each other in the classroom, followed by a single kiss after a slow dance at the sixth-form disco. If only it hadn't been raining...

Although Tom's flirtatious comments had ceased after she'd gone home in Rob's car, she had still been aware of his longing gaze when he thought she wasn't looking. She should have told him she'd only accepted Rob's lift so that the rain wouldn't ruin her new rope-soled wedge sandals. They had cost her a month's wages. Not long after, she'd given the shoes to her younger sister.

Next time the dentist touched her cavity, she managed to stay still.

"So how did the old filling become dislodged?" His tone was so casual, he might as well have been asking

18

where she was going for her holidays. (The answer would have been nowhere. Again.)

"Muesli," she replied quickly, having scrubbed her teeth extra hard before she left home to get rid of any incriminating evidence of chocolate.

From the way his eyes crinkled, she guessed he was smiling behind his mask. Tom's eyes used to crease like that when he smiled.

"Excellent choice. Healthy and sustaining. I have porridge for breakfast every day myself. Stops my tummy rumbling in my patients' ears." He patted his stomach, taut beneath his mauve tunic. Dr Parsons could have done with a lesson from him. "Although I confess to croissants at the weekends, with fresh fruit in season. And prosecco, of course. Do you think prosecco counts as one of my five a day?"

Juliet smiled around the probe. Could there be a more romantic breakfast? Shared with the right person, of course. She only ever bought croissants when they were reduced for quick sale, and they never fulfilled their promise. As for prosecco, Rob would want his in a pint mug.

"Looks pretty straightforward to me, Mrs Morris," the dentist was saying. "We'll fix that for you in no time. How would you feel if we numb the area first?"

She was grateful that he avoided the word "injection" to make it less scary. Tom had always been considerate, too.

"OK, yes, thank you." Her voice came out shrill. She closed her eyes so as not to see the needle, trying to think of waves gently lapping at a Mediterranean beach of fine golden sand. Were there waves on the Mediterranean? She had a suspicion it wasn't tidal.

"Now, what I need you to do next is to concentrate on wiggling your toes."

How strange, thought Juliet. Maybe that makes the anaesthetic work faster. The foot bone's connected to the leg bone, as in the old song, but did the nerves in her toes really run all the way to her jaw? Biology had never been her forte.

"Keep wiggling those toes." His masterful tone ensured she obeyed. Only after he had withdrawn the needle did she realise that the toe-wiggling routine was simply a psychological distraction from the needle. Tom always had been clever, too.

After a few moments, the dentist checked the injection had been effective before picking up the drill and setting to work. As the nurse moved in with the vacuum, Juliet relived her memories of Tom and her regrets. Thinking about their one kiss diverted her as the filling took shape.

When the dentist leaned closer to inspect his handiwork, she began to worry about how different she looked thirty years on from their last encounter. Even if this really was Tom Jenkinson, he probably wouldn't recognise her. Her surname wasn't the only thing about her that had changed since their schooldays. Around her

20

once slender midriff clung a thick layer of fat, which Rob jokingly called her life-preserver. Might her stomach look flatter while she was lying down in the dentist's chair? Would gravity make the surplus flesh fall back against the seat, like a resting beanbag?

Gravity could also be kind to her face. Horizontal, she might look like the after-shot of a facelift. She wished Jessie had got round to doing that eyebrow shape she kept promising.

"There we are, Mrs Morris, all done!" With a forefinger, the dentist gave the gentlest caress to her cheek. His first medically unnecessary touch made Juliet shiver with pleasure. At least she still had her high cheekbones. Her friend Maisie had always envied them.

The dentist cleared his throat. "Now, don't eat on that side for the next two hours." He glanced at the wall clock. "So not before 3pm. I hope that's not going to scupper your plans for a hot lunch date, Mrs Morris?"

His eyes twinkled above his mask.

Juliet pictured Rob, sitting in his work van, chewing his packed lunch with his mouth open.

As she replied, her numb upper jaw made her slur her words. "The closest thing I've got to a hot date this afternoon is to take my husband's car to be repaired."

Their car really, but like everything they owned, it was registered in Rob's name. He preferred it that way, and she preferred to avoid arguments.

Inwardly, she cursed herself for letting slip she had a husband. Although the dentist had addressed her as Mrs,

21

for all he knew, she might be widowed or divorced. Not that she considered herself available. She'd made her marital bed and she would lie on it, lumpy and uncomfortable though it may be.

The dentist pressed the floor pedal to raise the back of the chair to vertical. Juliet swung her legs round to place her feet on the floor, slightly dizzy from the sudden change of position. As she held on to the arm of the chair to steady herself, she became aware that the dentist was watching her surreptitiously, just as Tom had done all those years ago in the classroom. Pretending not to notice, she stood up, put on her coat, fumbled with her bag and dropped her keys on the floor. Without looking at the dentist again, she picked them up and headed for the door, mumbling her gratitude.

Just before she left the room, the dentist spoke again.

"Bye, Gems, take care."

Gems, the more flattering nickname Tom Jenkinson had given her at school, aware that she hated Jools. Once, when she wasn't looking, he had graffitied on the cover of her rough notebook: "Jools > Jewels > Gems", illustrated with a line drawing of a huge multi-faceted diamond.

When Juliet turned to reply, the dentist was already at his computer, his back to her once more, summoning up his next patient's records. Had she imagined that last comment? Dental treatment always did make her feel a bit odd, almost out-of-body.

She stumbled down the stairs to settle the bill at reception, where the air was thick with the lingering aroma of disinfectant, but it was the new dentist's expensive cologne that held her senses in thrall.

3 Mrs Dent

"Look out, lads, it's Mrs Dent!"

Juliet usually took the mechanics' teasing nickname in good heart. Responding with a wry smile was easier than telling them who was really responsible for the damage that made her their most frequent customer. It wasn't as if anyone important was within range to hear them.

But today, still numb from the dental anaesthetic, she didn't want to smile for fear of frightening them with her half-paralysed face. Her lopsided look might make them think she'd had a stroke and leap on her to apply first aid. She hoped the lack of feeling wouldn't make her drool. Jools to rhyme with drools, said an annoying voice in her head.

As she reversed neatly into the parking bay closest to the mechanics' workshop, light raindrops dappled the windscreen. She slipped the gearstick into neutral.

"I'm an excellent driver," she said to herself, engaging the handbrake.

She often wanted to say this to Rob during his running commentaries on the faults in her driving. She'd never had a motoring accident, nor even touched an unintended object with her bumper. But she knew he'd simply retort, "Yeah, so was Rain Man."

They'd seen the film on a date before they were married. She'd chosen it to appeal to him, as it featured a fancy car and a road-trip, but Rob had completely missed its point, aligning himself with the young Tom Cruise before he saw the light about his autistic brother.

She switched off the engine, but before getting out of the car, she glanced in the rear-view mirror. The anaesthetic had now reached her temple, causing the odd tear to leak out and smudge her mascara. She licked a forefinger and ran it under each eye. Then, grabbing her handbag, she braced herself to face the mischievous mechanics.

Or Santa's elves, as she liked to think of them, to make them seem less threatening. The analogy was obvious. Dave, their boss, had a long beard and hair of astonishing whiteness for a man who spent his days in an atmosphere redolent of motor oil. Juliet secretly wondered whether he used the purple shampoo her grey-haired friends raved about, and which reminded her of the Reckitt's Blue Bags her grandma used in her old twin-tub. She touched her fading hair. She'd need purple shampoo herself soon.

Dave's beard fell in soft waves almost to his navel, making Juliet wonder whether he plaited it before bed, as she used to do to Jessie's hair when she was little. It was fun unleashing the neat zigzags every morning.

As she headed for the office to drop off Rob's car key, Dave came out to meet her on the forecourt, sparing her from entering the mechanics' lair. Juliet felt rude for not returning Dave's welcoming smile, but her paralysed cheek would not cooperate.

"Hello, hello," he said cheerily, greeting her with the familiarity of an old friend. Juliet couldn't remember when Rob had first introduced her to Dave or how he had found out about his service, tucked away off the main drag here, but she felt as if he'd always been a part of their lives. Dave was seventy if he was a day, but he seemed the type who would never retire.

As Juliet opened her mouth to return his greeting, the tingling in her lips suggested she'd be unable to speak clearly, so she decided to keep conversation to the minimum.

"Hello, Dave." She raised a hand to the numb side of her face. To her embarrassment, a tear fell on her fingertip. She brushed it away, hoping to pass it off as a raindrop.

Dave's voice was as gentle as his beard was soft.

"You don't want to take any notice of my lads. Just tell me what the trouble is, and I'll have it fixed for you in no time."

"The trouble?"

"The damage. To the car."

He stroked the tip of his white beard, as if encouraging it to grow even longer. Juliet wondered whether his beard ever became entangled in car engines. Perhaps he should keep it out of harm's way in a hairnet, like the young man behind the counter of the local bakery.

Unnerved by her silence, Dave tried again.

"Another accident, or something else this time?"

Juliet chose her words carefully to avoid lisping.

"A broken rear lamp, actually. Back left."

Dave nodded sympathetically. "I suppose it was the turn of the nearside rear. At least you'll have a nice new lamp now to match the other three. You're nothing if not fair-minded, Mrs Dent."

His hand flew to his mouth in remorse for using the mechanics' disrespectful nickname. Any other day, Juliet would have waved away his error, but now, with both her tongue and upper lip devoid of sensation, she felt no responsibility for the words they formed and began to speak her mind.

"Why does no-one ever use my proper name these days?" As she said it, she realised she had lost all feeling in the tip of her tongue. How could the effect of the anaesthetic still be increasing? In another hour, she was meant to be able to eat and drink again. "And by the way, if I am Mrs Dent, it's only because I stupidly married Mr Dent. No, make that Lord Dent, master of reckless driving, who blames all his stupid accidents on me. Surely you must have realised by now that my husband

27

is responsible for this broken lamp, and all the other damage that he makes me bring to you for repair. It's bad enough wasting my day off hanging around in town while you fix it, without having to bear the blame for the wreckage as well. I'm an excellent driver, and I have a clean record to prove it."

Dave raised his hands to stem her indignation.

"That's fine, love, I believe you. You don't need to show me your driving licence to convince me."

Which was just as well, because Juliet's licence was endorsed with six points for speeding, offences committed by Rob, but which he had cajoled her into accepting on his behalf. His licence was already maxed out, and she wouldn't want him to be unable to drive for work, would she?

Juliet chewed her lip, though it had no feeling.

"I'm sorry, love, you must think me stupid. I thought you were a very tidy parker for someone who'd had so many prangs." He curled his fingers around the end of his beard, pulling it into a tight bunch. "I shall have to have words with your other half."

He's not my other half, thought Juliet crossly. I am a whole person.

Dave clearly hoped her silence meant she accepted his apology.

"Now, love, what can I do to make it up to you? Knock a bit off the bill today?"

Juliet welcomed the opportunity for speedy reconciliation, but wanted it on her terms.

28

"It's not me who pays the repair bills. That would only be compensating Rob." When they married, they'd agreed that Rob would pay the mortgage and motoring costs, while Juliet's salary would cover household bills and groceries.

Dave glanced around the forecourt for inspiration.

"I know, you can borrow my special loan car for the afternoon." He pointed to the corner of the yard at a gleaming Mini the same shade of purple as a Cadbury's Dairy Milk wrapper, Juliet's favourite colour. "I keep this car for my special customers. Why not treat yourself to a nice drive out into the country for the afternoon instead of killing time in town?"

Juliet gazed at the Mini. It was just like the one she'd bought after passing her driving test. But this car was the modern model, with twenty-first century gadgets and trimmings. Trying them out might be rather fun. Dave was right, a little drive in the country would cheer her up. At this time of year, once you got out of town, the country lanes looked gorgeous, with trees in full bright leaf, hedgerows bursting with May blossom and Queen Anne's lace. Rob called it cow parsley when uprooting it in their back garden, but he hadn't yet sapped all the romance out of life.

She began to regain sensation in her tongue.

"Thanks, Dave, I think I'd enjoy that very much."

Visibly relieved, Dave produced a key fob from his bib pocket.

"It's a fun little motor, all right," said Dave, leading her over to the Mini. "Just turn on the satnav, press the option marked 'scenic route' and follow the instructions. You'll have a lovely drive, even in the rain. Then press 'home' when you've had enough."

She assumed that would bring her back to his garage.

Dave's unexpected kindness made her lower lip crumple like a bumper against a lamp post. Another tear streaked past her guard.

"I've just been to the dentist."

Her voice was as high as a schoolgirl's. Dave folded his arms as if to stop himself giving her a comforting hug.

"You can keep the car until tomorrow morning, if you like. No-one else is down to use it until 11 o'clock."

Bigger raindrops began to rebound from the tarmac. Juliet wiped one from the end of her nose with the back of her hand.

"OK, Dave, thanks. I'll be careful with it, I promise."

"I know you will, love. Have fun."

Before she could change her mind, Juliet clicked the central locking button on the smart key. The Mini's lights winked at her cheekily, as if pleased to see her. She smiled.

Dave was right. A little spin in this smart car would make a world of difference to how she was feeling.

She needn't tell Rob about her unexpected outing. He'd only complain that Dave would bump up the bill to cover the cost of her joyride. It would be her and Dave's little secret.

As Juliet turned on the ignition, the satnav screen lit up, and she reached out to press the button marked 'scenic route'. This was the me-time she'd been craving, and she planned to make the most of it while she could.

4 Mrs Jenkinson

As she followed the satnav's instructions and headed for the ring road, Juliet enjoyed the admiring glances from pedestrians envious of her beautiful car. It was so easy to drive, slipping from one gear to the next as smoothly as a spoon through cream.

The satnav's deep, suave tones made the journey feel even smoother. "Turn left and follow the road until you reach open fields. Be sure to notice the stand of historic old oaks on your right with the afternoon sun glinting through their leaves."

What a sophisticated commentary, thought Juliet. It was like having her own tour guide in the passenger seat. Rob's satnav gave the bare minimum of instructions.

She recalled Jessie, aged five, asking her earnestly about the man who managed Rob's satnav. Jessie had been under the impression that a real live person, in radio contact from some distant map room, was tracking the car wherever it went. She'd drawn a picture of them at a video screen in the tall RAC Control Tower beside the M5, which they'd passed on a day-trip to Weston-super-Mare.

Juliet smiled, wishing Jessie could see this fancy satnav. Built into the dashboard, it was much more sophisticated than Rob's clip-on one. Its image of the road was not a conventional digitised map, but in the style of a meticulous watercolour painting.

Juliet remembered how excited Rob had been when he'd bought his first satnav. He'd made excuses to drive to places he didn't know, supposedly to reconnoitre new neighbourhoods for his plastering business, but really only to spend more time with his new best friend: the man inside the satnav. But it wasn't long before Rob lost interest and stuck him on mute. He'd never liked being given instructions, preferring to lose his way rather than admit to needing help.

He was a funny old stick, her Rob. She supposed he must love her, although she couldn't remember the last time he'd said so. But it was not in the way she wanted to be loved. She took one hand from the steering wheel and stroked her cheek, just as the new dentist had done earlier. The feeling in her face was starting to come back.

"Take the next left, please, sweetheart," the satnav was saying. "Oh, and don't worry about turning the wipers off now the rain is easing. Let me do that for you."

Sure enough, the windscreen wipers paused without Juliet's help. As the sun came out from behind a dark cloud, the raindrops on the windscreen beyond the reach of the wipers' arc glistened like diamonds.

This satnav chappie was certainly taking good care of her. As he directed her to turn on to a road that ran alongside a pretty shaded stream, she realised how familiar his voice was, so deep and warm. Was this car so advanced that it could provide the kind of satnav voice you liked best without you even having to choose? A voice like her new dentist's. A voice like Tom Jenkinson's. How did it know?

No, that was ridiculous. The dental injection must have confused her brain. If this was how a trip to the dentist was going to affect her, she'd better start flossing more regularly. She always flossed for at least a week after every dental appointment, hoping to put off the need for another visit for as long as possible.

She turned right beside an ancient apple orchard, gnarled boughs heavy with pale pink blossom, and joined a single-track tree-lined lane so narrow that clouds of Queen Anne's lace beneath the hedgerows gently brushed both sides of the car, like long fingertips in lace gloves. There were no buildings in any direction, not even a barn.

As the lane passed through a wood, she pressed the button to scroll down the window, inhaling the heady scent of bluebells. She was glad to catch them in flower. For too many years, she'd missed their brief season, seldom venturing into the countryside just for the pleasure of immersing herself in nature.

Now and again, isolated old farmhouses came into view, clearly no longer home to farmers. Here was an upmarket bed and breakfast, there was one divided into holiday apartments, offering glamping in its spacious grounds. Then came a deconsecrated church, reincarnated as an art gallery and bistro.

There's money round here, thought Juliet. She'd long ago given up coveting houses larger than their three-bed turn-of-the-century terrace, but it hadn't stopped her occasionally fantasising about something more luxurious, especially after reading family sagas of the landed gentry or raunchy romances about self-made billionaires who fell for their secretaries. Working in the library, she'd never meet a billionaire.

As the road narrowed, Juliet shifted slightly in her seat, glad to be in a car with a tiny footprint. She was amazed how quickly she'd got used to the Mini. Usually she took a couple of days to adapt to one of Rob's new cars. New to them, anyway. They'd never owned a brand-new vehicle. Rob said new cars lost a couple of grand from their value as soon as you drove them off the showroom forecourt. Only people with more money – or debt – than sense drove new cars. That was one thing they agreed on.

The Mini was dead comfy, too. She must have been driving for nearly an hour now, but she didn't feel at all stiff or cramped. Maybe she could persuade Rob to buy a Mini next time he wrote his car off, especially as they no longer needed space for the kids.

Her reverie was interrupted by the satnav's further instructions.

"Please turn right in twenty metres – ten – now." She obeyed him instantly. "Arriving at destination," he announced, as they entered a long gravel drive concealed behind a glossy holly hedge. "Well driven."

"Thank you," replied Juliet, flushing with pleasure at the unaccustomed compliment.

She peered through the windscreen at the detached Edwardian villa that stood in front of her. With the air and scale of an old vicarage, it had damp walls and roof steaming slightly in the sudden burst of bright sunshine. Immediately in front of the house lay a turning circle made from an old millstone, surrounded by Cotswold stone blocks fitting together like perfect teeth. From the centre of the millstone bubbled a fountain shot through with tiny rainbows.

Feeling conspicuous in the purple Mini, Juliet checked the house for outward signs of life. Through the huge bay window at the front, she spotted a study. Against the far wall stood a substantial antique roll-top desk crowned with family photographs. Fortunately, no-one was working at it, so with luck, she might escape before anyone accused her of trespassing.

But why had the satnav sent her here? Surely Dave's scenic route wouldn't lead his customers into private gardens? Maybe this was the home of the last person to borrow the courtesy car. She checked the satnav screen for evidence, but it simply stated in an elegant cursive script, "Congratulations, you have reached your destination".

Maybe she had inadvertently pressed the "home" button and this was Dave's home. Could a motor repair business really pay for a fancy property like this? If so, Rob was in the wrong job.

Juliet was glad the turning circle precluded the need for a three-point turn. Not that she had any problems with reversing, but on this gravel, driving forward would be a little less noisy. The sooner she got out of here, the better.

As she was about to pull away, she had to switch her right foot swiftly from the accelerator to the brake, because just turning in from the lane was another car. The sleek silver Lexus drew to a halt in front of her, entirely blocking her exit from the turning circle, whether she drove forward or backwards.

In her confusion, Juliet forgot to return the gearstick to neutral, and the car kangarooed forward and stalled. She couldn't remember the last time she had stalled a car. Whoever was driving the Lexus, she'd given him a two-fold reason to tell her off – trespassing and bad driving.

The door of the Lexus swung open with a silent expensive action, and a tall, broad-shouldered man, the car's only occupant, stepped out. Cowering in the low-slung seat of the Mini, Juliet avoided eye contact, gazing instead at his immaculate midnight-blue suede shoes. He closed the door behind him and stepped nimbly around the fountain to open her door for her. Not wanting to be at a psychological disadvantage, she unclipped her seatbelt and prepared to get out of the car. As she swung her feet onto the gravel, the man reached down a strong hand to aid her, and she took it automatically. He pulled her up to her full height, so she stood facing him, inches away from his firm chest.

"Hello, darling, I see you beat me home. Well done."

When Thomas Jenkinson bent to kiss her full on the mouth, Juliet realised with growing delight that the dental anaesthetic had now entirely worn off. What's more, other feelings that had lain dormant deep inside for a very long time were flooding back as if they'd never been away.

5 Gems

The longer their kiss continued, the weaker was Juliet's desire to flee.

I can't drive away in any case, she told herself. Not with his Lexus in the way. I could just leg it, but I can't abandon Dave's Mini. It must be worth at least 20 grand. Besides, I'm in the middle of nowhere, and I don't know how to get back into town. That's the trouble with satnavs – trusting them to look after you diminishes your own navigation skills. I'll never get a signal on my mobile out here, so I can't depend on that for directions. Anyway, running would be pointless. With those long legs, he'd catch up with me in no time. He's obviously in good shape. Besides, gravel is hell to run on, as unstable beneath your feet as a stony beach. Better to cooperate than fall flat on my face.

Only when she was short of breath did she pull back from Tom's embrace and hold him at arms' length. When he fixed his big brown eyes on hers, his smile sent a thrill right through her, just as it had all those years ago at the school disco. At the start of her favourite romantic song of the moment, they'd moved towards each other like magnets, wrapping their arms around each other for a slow dance that was over far too quickly and ended with a kiss.

Kissing him now felt like a homecoming, but the whole encounter seemed bizarre. Maybe she'd received an accidental overdose of anaesthetic and was lying unconscious in the dentist's chair. If so, she couldn't be held accountable for her actions, nor feel guilty about kissing him back. Was it even possible to get an overdose of dental anaesthetic?

Before she could gather her thoughts, Tom took Juliet firmly by the hand and led her to the front door. He slid his key into the lock and ushered her across the threshold before closing the door behind them.

Inside the entrance hall, Juliet hesitated. She could only guess the layout of the house, a one-off design, standing in its own grounds. On the estate where she and Rob lived, every house had been built to the same plan. Once you'd been in one, you knew your way round every home in the street.

To buy time, she stooped to pick up the newspaper from the doormat.

"Let's have a coffee on the terrace before anything else," Tom was saying. "I'm parched. That drop of rain has perked everything up except me."

Coffee on the terrace: she could say yes to that with a clear conscience, even if it did seem a waste of dreamtime that might be spent more pleasurably. If she wasn't dreaming, it was a safe and blameless way to spend time with her old flame. Perhaps a spot of caffeine might help her get a grip on herself.

"That would be lovely."

As she followed Tom down the long hall to the kitchen, she hoped he'd make the coffee, because she had no idea how to work the fancy chrome-plated machine on the vast acreage of black marble worktop. While pretending to read the newspaper headlines, she watched him fill the water tank and drop in a foil pod for each cup. He fetched a carton of milk from a big red American-style fridge and steamed a jug full to add to their coffee. Then, dependent as a puppy, she trotted after him through the dining room, its walls lined with huge studio portraits of a boy and a girl at various stages of their childhood through to their early teens. They continued through a huge palm-filled conservatory, where Tom opened French doors on to a broad flagstoned terrace. Around the edge, silvery sage and acidbright basil spilled out of Etruscan stone pots.

Tom set the hand-thrown pottery mugs of coffee on a low table between two sturdy teak steamer chairs. Juliet wondered whether he ever went on cruises for his holidays. She'd always fancied a cruise.

"So, we have a couple of hours to kill before my parents arrive."

"Your parents?"

Juliet brightened. She hadn't allowed herself to think Tom might really be a crazed killer bent on abducting her, but she was glad to consider that a crazed killer would be unlikely to invite his parents over to watch him attack her.

"At least this week you don't have to worry about cooking for them. They'll be touched to know Eleanor made that casserole for them when she was home from school last weekend, and Edward the sorbet and shortbread." Tom paused to sip his coffee, emitting a satisfied sigh at first taste. "I think the new weekly boarding arrangement is really suiting the kids. It's the best of both worlds: plenty of opportunities to learn new practical skills alongside their academic studies and sports, while we get weekday evenings to ourselves, followed by quality family time at weekends."

Juliet stared into her coffee. So Tom's children were still at school? With his long training as a dentist, he must have come to parenthood later than she had. He probably married much later, too. A wave of nostalgia for her younger dependent children washed over her, and the days when they still believed she was perfect and all-knowing and weren't shy of expressing their love for her. Did Tom appreciate how lucky he was? If so, why on earth was he farming his kids out to strangers five days a week? Even if Juliet had been rich, she'd never have sent her kids away from home for such a large part of their childhood. It passed far too quickly.

But if the fancy studio portraits in the dining room were anything to go by, the children seemed happy enough. Beautiful, too, with gleaming dark curls, Tom's conker-coloured eyes and, of course, perfectly spaced white teeth.

"Yes, best of both worlds." Tom set down his mug. "So, what say you we take advantage of one of those benefits right now?" He sprang up from his armchair, all energy where moments ago had been only languor. "Come on, Gems."

Gently, he prised her mug from her and set it down on the table, before taking both her hands to haul her out of her seat. Juliet offered no resistance, thinking he'd probably not take no for an answer. A moment later, he was leading her back through the dining room, into the hall and towards the stairs.

6 Mummy

At the foot of the stairs, Juliet pulled her hand free.

"Before I do anything else, I just need to make a quick phone call." She hoped her voice sounded light and carefree, although her stomach was churning.

Tom was starting to undo his tie.

"OK, Gems, but don't keep me waiting long."

She watched him stride up the stairs two at a time, trying not to picture him undressing when he reached the bedroom. Then she opened the door to the study. Earlier, she had spotted a phone on the roll-top desk. Standing by the desk now, she raised the receiver, listening for tell-tale clicks in case Tom had decided to eavesdrop from the handset in the bedroom. It was the sort of house that would have handsets all over the place.

Having made herself comfortable on the leather captain's chair at the desk, Juliet dialled Rob's mobile number, swivelling round to survey the room. In an alcove beyond the open fireplace stood a slim antique oak bureau with a pull-down flap. On top of the bureau were more framed family photos, the largest of which was of Tom, sun-kissed and smiling in a lifejacket, in action on a sailing yacht. His plain white t-shirt beneath the custard-yellow lifejacket reflected the brilliance of the cloudless azure sky. One hand on the tiller, he was gazing with obvious affection at the photographer – perhaps one of his children? The smile was paternal rather than lustful.

Juliet swivelled back to examine the snaps on top of Tom's desk. Bracing herself to see the lucky woman that was Tom's real wife, she nearly dropped the phone when she spotted a headshot of herself.

For a moment, she thought it must be a mirror, but this was no reflection. It was Juliet as she would have been, had she lost a couple of stone – or rather, never gained it in middle-age. Her hair was its former auburn glory, her skin glowed beneath the Mediterranean sun.

Juliet had never even had a passport.

Maybe Tom had married her double. She'd once read in one of her library books a Ray Bradbury short story about a teenager, thwarted in his love for a beautiful high-school teacher, who goes on to marry a woman exactly like her, but his own age. Perhaps Tom had found someone else who looked just like Juliet, only in better shape.

Another explanation crossed her mind. Perhaps this whole thing was an elaborate practical joke. At any minute, a camera crew would leap out from behind the emerald velvet curtains that framed the bay window. Framed – yes, that was the right word: she'd been framed. It was the sort of heartless stunt a reality television programme might attempt, testing whether an old flame could tempt a woman to be unfaithful to her husband. Reality TV wasn't renowned for its kindness.

With no answer from Rob's mobile, she searched for further clues as to her double's identity. She crossed the mantlepiece to examine official school photos of Eleanor and Edward. Both had Tom's dark colouring, but their smile was strangely like her own. Despite their distinctive private school uniform with braid-edged blazer and stripey tie – none of the two-for-a-fiver supermarket specials that Jessie and Jake had worn throughout their schooldays – they looked relaxed, confident and neat. These were a far cry from her own kids' school photos. Jake always pulled a stupid expression as the shutter clicked, and Jessie's dishevelled curls made her look as if she'd just been turning cartwheels in a cloudburst.

Between the school photos were pictures of Tom's parents. They'd aged a bit since she last saw them on A Level results day, but they looked pretty good for their age. They'd always had plenty of money. No wonder they'd aged so gracefully.

Beside them was a photo of – surely not! – her own mother, looking ten years younger, with Tom's kids as toddlers holding her hands. Why had Tom kept in touch with her mother, but not with Juliet? Why hadn't her mother told her she'd been seeing him? She had always preferred Tom to Rob, but nurturing a secret relationship with him after Juliet's marriage was downright weird.

The thought of Rob reminded her to try their home number. He should have been back from work by now.

While she waited for him to pick up, she examined a sweet little photo on top of Tom's desk of herself holding a baby in pink pyjamas. Edward, looking about two, stood at her side, holding the baby's fingers in one hand, his other hand on Juliet's thigh. The baby must be Eleanor.

But if Juliet was the mother of Tom's children, as these photos suggested, what had become of Jessie and Jake? If it wasn't for the thought of them as she dialled her landline, she'd have been hoping for an unobtainable signal. There was a certain logic to her train of thought. If she'd married Tom instead of Rob, Rob wouldn't be living in the house they'd bought as newlyweds, and their landline of the last thirty years wouldn't exist.

If the line was dead, could she really relax with a clear conscience and proceed with Tom's plans for their evening? And maybe for the rest of her life? How strange it would seem to meet Edward and Eleanor at the weekend when they came home from school and called her Mum.

The thought of Jessie and Jake decided her. If Rob answered the phone, she would go back to him. It would be unthinkable to abandon their children.

Her pulse quickened as the ringing tone sounded. Rob picked up almost immediately.

"'Lo. Who's that?"

Juliet sighed so hard that for a moment, she feared she'd sound like a heavy breather.

"It's me, Juliet."

"Oh, hi, Jools. Make it quick, Sam's at the door and we're about to head to The Fleece for a jar or three."

She paused, disconcerted by Rob's apparent disregard for her absence. She should have been home, with the repaired car, two hours before. Why wasn't he worried about her? Why wasn't he glad to hear her voice as proof that she was safe? Had he even noticed she was gone?

"Maisie's mum's ill," she heard herself saying. "Maisie's asked me to stay with her tonight for moral support."

"What about my tea?"

"You can get a pie at the pub."

"And my packed lunch tomorrow?"

Juliet gazed at the huge photo over the fireplace before she responded.

"You can make it yourself," she said at last. "You're a grown-up. Once every thirty years is not a big ask."

In all their married life, Rob had never made her so much as a cup of tea.

"OK, bye, Jools. That's me gone now."

Gone for good? thought Juliet, with a shiver of mingled excitement and fear. Or just to the pub?

As the line went dead, she stared out of the window on to the forecourt. The Mini's metallic finish was sparkling in the low evening sun.

Juliet replaced the handset and went to examine the expensive canvas enlargement of a wedding day photograph which hung over the fireplace. Beneath a professional photographer's logo in the bottom right-hand corner, a date stamp told her the occasion was fifteen years ago. Tom was as handsome, poised and confident as ever, and his wife – his wife was herself.

My goodness, she looked radiant. Clearly no expense had been spared on the dress or the flowers, a lavish armful of lilies, and her hair and make-up had been done by professionals. In the background, surrounded by cherry trees in full bloom, was a pretty, ancient church, and around them a pool of rose petal confetti lay at their feet.

The overall effect was far showier than Juliet would have chosen, so different from her modest wedding with Rob, a low-budget civil ceremony in Cirencester Register Office above the library, then back to a room over the pub for a meal with close family and friends. Juliet bet Tom's wedding reception hadn't been in a room above a pub.

Tom's wedding – and hers. For now she realised that she was living the life she would have led, had she married Tom.

7 My Wife

"My wife!" whispered Tom, waking Juliet from her contented slumber.

Juliet's eyes snapped open like a roller blind whose cord has been pulled too hard. She struggled out of Tom's arms, which he'd draped gently about her as she slept. For a moment, she assumed he was sounding the alarm at the unexpected arrival of his spouse, now about to catch them naked in bed together. As she pulled the duvet up to her chin, Tom propped himself up on one elbow and gazed down at her.

"Is that such an awful title, Gems? I thought you'd be used to it after all this time." He smiled. "To be honest, there are still times when I can't get over my good fortune at marrying you, but I didn't mean to say it aloud."

Juliet let go of the duvet and rolled over to face him, snuggling into his bare chest, breathing in his cologne. Rob always wore an old t-shirt and trackie bottoms in bed these days. The closest he ever got to cologne was shower gel, on a good day.

"Nor can I," Juliet murmured truthfully.

"Many girls wouldn't have waited for me to finish my studies and get my first job in practice before I proposed. Still, it could have been worse. If I'd trained as a doctor, you'd have had to wait even longer, and my working hours would be much more anti-social."

Juliet wasn't sure what to say. He took her silence as a signal to continue.

"Not that I mind doing one weekend a month on the emergency rota or the odd locum duty. It would have been selfish not to cover for George Allsop today. He's been waiting months for that hospital appointment, and it was easy enough for me to fill in for him, what with my treatment room being out of action while the new chair is being installed."

Tom wriggled up into a sitting position, rested his broad back against the nut-brown padded leather headboard and gazed across at the huge bay window. Immediately above the study, it gave on to views of gently rolling hills beyond the top of the holly hedge.

"Oh well, back to the grind among the dreaming spires tomorrow." He grinned at his dental pun. Juliet wondered whether he made it every working day.

So Oxford was where he usually worked. No wonder she'd not seen him around Cirencester. She guessed his house must be in some posh remote hamlet near Witney or Burford. Very nice too.

As Juliet sat up beside him, Tom lowered an arm around her shoulders.

"You know, sometimes I think it would be nice to spend a whole day together midweek while the children are at school, but my budget won't quite run to that yet. Not until at least one of the mortgages is paid off."

One of the mortgages? thought Juliet. Despite the unfortunate business with the taxman, she and Rob had only ever had a single mortgage, and they'd paid that off a few years before.

"On the plus side, apart from work, we've another twenty-four hours to ourselves."

And another sixteen hours before I have to return Dave's loan car, thought Juliet. Returning the car would most likely break the spell, and she didn't want to do it before it had to be broken.

Deciding to make the most of those sixteen hours, she reached her arm across Tom's chest and attempted to pull him back down beneath the covers. He grabbed her hand and raised it to his lips.

"I'm sorry, darling, but that's your ration for now. Don't forget my folks will be round at 7 for 7.30, as it's a Thursday. And it's gone six already. We'd better get up and get busy."

Feeling out of her depth, Juliet glanced at the nightstand, where a small square antique alarm clock caught her eye. Its beautiful Art Deco design folded down into a tan leather case. She wondered where its original owner had taken it on her travels. On the Orient

Express? The *Queen Mary*? The sleeper to the Scottish Highlands? It looked better travelled than she was.

She wondered what Tom meant by "getting busy". Just heating up Eleanor's casserole wouldn't take much effort, or must they do more? What would Tom's parents expect of her? She couldn't remember much about them from their few brief encounters in the school car park, other than a general impression of their affluence. Their elite saloon cars made the teachers' hatchbacks look shabby and small. She'd only ever seen Tom's father in an immaculate business suit, and his mother always looked as if she'd just stepped out of the hairdresser's.

Watching Tom swing his sturdy legs out of the bed and heave himself upright distracted her. How did a dentist develop such strong thigh muscles? Dentistry wasn't exactly sedentary, but nor was it physically demanding, not in a bodybuilding way. Maybe wheeling himself about on that funny little stool all day, from computer to treatment chair, helped develop his leg muscles. Maybe that was why he did it, rather than from laziness.

From the mirror-fronted wardrobes that lined the left wall of the bedroom, Tom pulled white boxer shorts, soft buff chinos and a shirt patterned in a tiny pink sprig that would make the rest of him seem all the more manly. Rob would have died of embarrassment if she'd made him wear a floral shirt. T-shirts, jeans and fleeces were all the clothes he possessed.

"Come on, Gems, look lively. If you get dressed quickly, we'll have time to enjoy a cocktail on the terrace before Mother and Father arrive."

Whistling jauntily, with the clean clothes draped over his arm, he headed for their bathroom – a rather nice en suite, Juliet noticed with satisfaction.

Listening to the shower drumming as loud as a tropical rainstorm, Juliet leaned back against the headboard to think. If Tom was convinced she was his wife, it was an illusion she was willing to humour, at least until she had to return the Mini to Dave the next day. First she was looking forward to getting to know his parents. Tom must have got his easy charm from them.

But wait! Why hadn't he mentioned filling her tooth, even if only to check she was OK? She'd half expected him to take advantage of her being horizontal again to admire his handiwork. Surely he hadn't forgotten?

Perhaps there had been a leak in the gas cylinder in George Allsop's surgery. (Dentists did still use anaesthetic gas occasionally, didn't they?) As Tom was only standing in for the day, he might not have been familiar with the set-up. It would be all too easy to inadvertently switch something on that should have been off. An influx of gas might muddle his thinking, even if it didn't knock him right out. It was a miracle that he'd driven his Lexus home without mishap.

Was she also a victim of the gas leak? That would explain her confusion after the appointment. What she'd taken for watercolour images on the Mini's satnav might really have been psychedelic hallucinations. Exposed to the gas leak for just the duration of her appointment, Juliet would have got off lighter than Tom, whereas he might have been inhaling it all day.

The effect of the gas would also account for her lack of self-consciousness, first in standing up to Dave, and then in taking her middle-aged body to bed with Tom. There was at least half as much again of her as there had been when he had last seen her on A Level results day.

Sliding her hands defensively down to her waistline, she found, to her astonishment, that it felt much trimmer than usual. Gone was the circling roll of flesh that Rob liked to call her life-preserver. It wasn't just the effect of lying down, either. Where on earth had it gone? She pictured a roll of discarded fat lying in a ditch by the side of one of the lanes she'd driven down, like an abandoned mattress in a lay-by, or a pair of knickers with snapped elastic whose owner had stepped out of them and walked away. She hoped it hadn't fallen out on the drive when she'd opened her car door, or she'd have some explaining to do to her in-laws.

No, not her in-laws. Tom's parents. She was finding it harder and harder to resist the scenario he had painted for them. She'd always been easy to hoodwink. That's how she'd come to marry Rob.

She put one hand to her mouth for a comforting chew of a fingernail, but withdrew her finger in surprise at the unfamiliar smooth sensation against her tongue. She stared at her nails. Usually bitten down to the flesh, they were now neatly shaped and flawlessly painted rose-pink with the durable finish that comes only from paid-for professional manicures. A hand model would have been proud of them.

Tom emerged from the bathroom, damp hair neatly combed, still buttoning his floral shirt.

"Come on, lazy bones!" He tickled her toes as he passed. "I'll go and get the drinks in. Gin and tonic or margarita?"

His voice was relaxed and warm.

"Margarita, please."

Juliet waited until he was padding down the stairs before flinging back the duvet and getting out of bed.

So where did the Mini come in? She couldn't imagine that as Tom's wife, she'd be a customer of Dave's scruffy backstreet garage. Perhaps this was a ruse after all, and Tom had bribed Dave to send her to his house via a high-tech kind of kidnapping using the fancy satnav that spoke with his voice.

But Tom couldn't have known she was going to turn up at Mr Allsop's surgery. Her appointment was a last-minute emergency, not an advance booking. Even if Tom wanted to kidnap her, would he take the professional risk? He had always been a sensible, responsible type. He had been Head Boy. Seducing a patient, no matter how willing, would be professional misconduct and could cost him his career.

Or had she dreamed the Mini up too – and Rob and Jessie and Jake? Desperate now for evidence of her former life, she darted to the window to check on the forecourt. The Mini glinted back at her. Well, at least that was real.

The touch of the cold windowpane against her palm reminded her she was naked. Whether Tom was deranged, drugged or simply criminal, and whether either or both of them had amnesia, getting dressed could only help matters. And if his parents were coming to dinner, she'd better put on a smarter outfit than the one she'd arrived in.

She slid open the mirrored doors of the wardrobes lining the right wall to reveal an array of beautiful outfits arranged in rainbow order. At least if Tom's real wife turned up and Juliet got arrested for impersonation, she'd look good in the police mug shot.

Selecting an olive linen shift, she checked the label: two sizes smaller than her usual purchases, but when she tried it on, it was a perfect fit. As she slipped on peach-soft grey mules, she noticed with pleasure how well they set off her professionally pedicured toenails. Feeling more confident, she started down the stairs, lured by the tinkle of ice cubes in crystal glasses and Tom's footsteps heading through the dining room and on to the terrace.

Settled once more into his teak steamer chair, Tom had turned his face to the late evening sunshine. The tang of lime cut through the still air. Juliet licked her lips as she sat down beside him and picked up her drink from the coffee table.

The glass was halfway to her lips before she realised she hadn't seen Tom mix the drinks. Supposing he'd slipped in a sedative to erase her short-term memory? He'd probably have access to that kind of drug at work for clinical purposes.

Or the drink might be drug free, but very alcoholic. From her nights as a barmaid when the kids were small, she knew a standard sized margarita was two measures of tequila and one of Cointreau. This one was at least a double. Delicious, but enough to prevent her driving home.

"Cheers," Tom was saying, clinking his glass against hers.

"Cheers," she replied automatically.

If the drink was meant to loosen her inhibitions, wouldn't refusing it be rather shutting the stable door after the horse had bolted into the bedroom? Did it even matter? Dave had said she needn't bring the car back till the next morning.

Of course it mattered. She'd been unfaithful to Rob. It may have been a mistake to have married him in the first place, but he was her husband.

Furtively, she glanced at her partner in crime. He couldn't have looked less threatening if he'd tried. No, more so, his lean face having matured as much as his body, gaining character and expression, no longer a blank slate for his future to etch. The fine wrinkles at the corners of his eyes and mouth and the faint mesh of lines across his forehead gave him a stronger, more masculine air than in adolescence.

It seemed such a long time since she had married Rob. And even a murderer got time off for good behaviour.

She raised the margarita to her lips.

8 Dilly

It was fortunate that whoever had been playing the part of Tom's wife until now had a logical, tidy mind, because that made it easy for Juliet to find the cutlery and crockery for supper.

Juliet looked up from arranging the knives and forks as Tom came in from the garden via the conservatory.

"I suppose I'd better let the wine breathe. You know what a stickler Father is for the temperature of his red wine. Not that Mum cares a jot as long as she has her gin and tonic before supper."

As he strolled past her, he ran a finger affectionately down her spine and she shivered.

Standing back to check the place settings, Juliet decided the table needed something extra to finish it off. A trill of birdsong from the garden drew her attention to the curvaceous borders, immaculately weeded – they must surely have a gardener – and brimming with summer flowers ripe for plucking: roses, stocks, wallflowers and lavender. In the far corner stood lilac trees heavy with blossom.

She found a collection of vases in the oak dresser and selected a heavy cut-glass number with a splayed top that would allow lilac branches to spread out and exude their heady perfume into the warm evening air. Soon she'd filled it with a fistful of branches of deep purple lilac. The crevasses of the vase sparkled beneath the clusters of tiny petals.

"You're always so good at this," said Tom, returning from the cellar – yes, they had a cellar! – with a bottle of red wine in each hand.

Juliet wasn't used to receiving compliments. "Good at what?"

He produced a Swiss Army knife from his pocket and selected the corkscrew.

"Oh, you know, homemaking." With skill born of long practice, he eased the cork out of each bottle and set them open on a small silver tray. "I feel sorry for men whose wives are too distracted by their jobs to take care of them properly at home. I bet plenty of working women would swap places in a heartbeat with a lady of leisure like you."

A lady of leisure? Although Juliet had occasionally craved a sabbatical when the children were tiny or poorly, she'd never longed to give up work entirely. Even in a house as big and as comfortable as this, would it really be possible to fill her days without a paid job? Wouldn't she be lonely, especially with the children at boarding school? She loved her job at the library. How would she fill her time without it? Even she wouldn't be contented to read all day, every day.

Judging from the packed wardrobe she'd just raided, Tom's wife filled her free time with clothes-shopping.

Leaving Tom to choose the appropriate wine glasses from the backlit display cabinet, Juliet returned to the kitchen, lifted Eleanor's casserole out of the fridge and slipped it into the hottest oven of the Aga. She was grateful to Eleanor for making the evening's catering easy for her. Juliet had never used an Aga before. She wasn't sure she'd even seen one in real life, only in her mind's eye through the novels of Katie Fforde and Joanna Trollope, and in glossy lifestyle magazines at the hairdresser's.

Rummaging through the kitchen cupboards, she found appropriate serving dishes for the sorbet and shortbread. Goodness, having to sift through so many dishes made life unnecessarily more complicated than it needed to be. It was much easier in her own house, where they ate whatever was on the menu off the same sturdy crockery they'd had since they were married, using the same simple set of knives, forks and spoons. Now she had access to steak knives, fish knives and forks, and some long skewer-like gadgets that she could not identify.

The casserole had plenty of gravy. She decided to add soupspoons to the place settings to be on the safe side.

Returning to the dining room and straightening the crockery and cutlery on the table for the third time, she was conscious of her heart pounding, so she decided to put on a calming CD. In the rack beside the fancy wall-mounted player, she found Vivaldi's *Four Seasons*, an old favourite that always made her relax and went down well as background music for public events at the library. Candles were soothing, too. She fetched from the sideboard two large ones in decorative glasses with fancy brand labels she couldn't pronounce and set them beside the lilac, whose perfume was already filling the room.

Just then she heard a key at the front door. Puzzled, she glanced towards the garden, where Tom was strolling around the lawn, a glass of Scotch in one hand, a slender cigar in the other. She hadn't realised Tom smoked. He was never one of the gang smoking behind the bus stop after school.

Multiple footsteps in the hall told her more than one person had let themselves in. It could only be Tom's parents. Tingling with anticipation, Juliet took a deep breath.

"Tom, darling! We're here!"

Juliet was just wondering whether Tom had heard them when Mr and Mrs Jenkinson stalked into the dining room. For the first time, she realised how much Tom took after his mother in appearance, with her doe-like brown eyes and dark curls. But in Veronica, there was a harshness about her straight lips. Her cynical stare fell upon Juliet.

"Where's my dear boy?" she asked in a tone that blamed Juliet for his absence. Behind her, Tom's father Henry raised his eyebrows at Juliet in a helpless apology.

"He's in the garden." Juliet forced a conciliatory smile. "Shall we go out to join him? It's a beautiful evening."

Henry obediently started to make for the patio. Veronica paused to appraise the table setting and pointed accusingly at the vase.

"Don't you know it's bad luck to bring lilac indoors? It's a portent of death."

"I thought that was peacock feathers," Juliet ventured weakly.

Veronica rolled her eyes.

"I hope you've none of those either. And have you nothing better to spend Tom's money on than those extravagant candles?"

Juliet thought fast.

"They were a gift."

They might have been for all she knew.

Veronica inspected the CD player on the wall and sighed.

"I thought so. The piece chosen by everyone who knows nothing about classical music, but wants to make it look as if they do."

Juliet gritted her teeth to prevent herself answering back.

Hearing Veronica's strident tones, Tom flung his half-smoked cigar into the shrubbery and strolled up the lawn to the patio. As he entered the dining room, Veronica's demeanour changed entirely. Suddenly, she was all charm, just like Tom.

"Thomas, darling!"

"Hello, Mother." Veronica allowed her son to sweep her into his arms and kiss her on both cheeks.

Tom acknowledged Henry with a nod of the head.

"Father."

"Thomas."

Juliet was startled to realise this was the first word Henry had spoken since his arrival.

"Drinks on the terrace OK for you, Mother?" Tom led her by the arm like an ambassador escorting an elderly duchess into a banquet. "I've got your drinkies ready for you, just how you like them."

Tom had set up the makings of gin and tonic on a circular bottle-green cast-iron table, around which were ranged four matching chairs. It wasn't just any old gin and tonic, but fancy gins and upmarket mixers too posh for the pub Juliet had worked in.

While Henry followed his wife and son, Juliet lingered behind. She couldn't bear to discard the vase of lilac, so she took it upstairs to the master bedroom and placed it on the dressing table. At least when she and Tom went to bed, the room would be filled with the seductive fragrance: sweet revenge on Veronica. Putting off the moment when she had to join her in-laws in the garden, she returned to the kitchen to check on the casserole.

By the time she entered the garden, Juliet was more than ready for the generous drink Tom had poured for her.

"We're just talking about where to go on holiday this summer, darling," Tom said as she sat down beside him. "Father favours Tuscany, but Mother favours Bavaria. You know how much we all enjoyed the Rhine cruise last summer."

"But it is my turn to choose, darlings," put in Henry.

Wary of saying the wrong thing, Juliet let them continue their debate, which was a token argument. She soon gathered that wherever Veronica chose, Henry eventually accepted, and it was understood that Juliet, Tom and the children would go with them. It turned out they had spent every vacation together as an extended family group. When Edward was a baby, Veronica had announced her presence would give Tom and Juliet a rest, an argument repeated on Eleanor's arrival two years later. As Veronica and Henry had paid for every holiday, it had become a family tradition.

With Veronica still extolling the virtues of Munich, they moved inside to eat. Veronica and Henry sat at each end of the table, with Tom and Juliet on either side, as if they were guests rather than hosts. Juliet was grateful that the self-contained one-dish meal should make serving everyone relatively fool-proof.

As Juliet filled her mother-in-law's plate, Veronica picked up her soup spoon and held it aloft.

"Have you forgotten to bring the soup as a starter?" she demanded.

Juliet almost dropped the ladle in surprise. "No, there isn't any starter. The soup spoon is for Eleanor's casserole, along with the knife and fork. There's a lot of gravy."

"I see," said Veronica, in a tone that suggested she didn't. "So Eleanor made this casserole?"

"Yes," said Juliet, cautiously. "Yes, she made it for you."

Veronica brightened.

"Then I'm sure it will be delicious."

Compared to how it would have been had I cooked it? thought Juliet. Would the lilac have passed muster had Eleanor picked it, and the candles if a gift from Edward?

"So how are the little lambs getting on at school this week?" asked Henry as Juliet set his plate of casserole in front of him.

"Oh, fine," said Juliet quickly, hoping Tom would elaborate, but he wasn't listening, too preoccupied with tasting the red wine.

The reason for Henry's question soon became clear.

"We've had a very long email from each of them, haven't we, Henry?"

Tom smiled. "Sending you regular updates is the least they can do considering you're paying their fees, Mother. Although I'm sure they're also messaging you because they miss you."

He cast Juliet an encouraging smile.

Juliet thought quickly. "I don't know how anyone pays school fees without grandparents' help these days," was the most diplomatic thing she could find to say. Not that she had any idea how much private school fees cost. When Jessie and Jake were at school, forking out for uniforms, sports kit, book bags and other paraphernalia had been a significant drain on her budget, even buying everything from the supermarket.

"The weekly boarding seems to be paying off, Dilly," replied Veronica.

Juliet looked around, wondering how another woman had crept into the room uninvited and unnoticed, but she refused to let this Dilly person distract her from the fact that her mother-in-law had paid to remove her children from her care during term-time. Now was her chance to protest.

Henry sensed Juliet's disquiet before she could speak.

"Of course, we're glad to be able to do it for them," he put in. "We only wish we could have sent Tom to boarding school instead of that dreadful state comprehensive. No offence, Juliet, it probably suited you well enough. But he got there in the end. To a proper professional career, I mean."

Juliet remembered now that Henry was a very successful barrister, which was odd, considering he could scarcely stand up to his wife. As a teenager, Tom had told Juliet that there was no point in him visiting most of the stands at the school careers fair, as his parents had declared the only routes open to him were the professions: law, medicine, dentistry, engineering, or accountancy. What about teaching? the careers advisor had asked him. Or librarianship? Juliet suggested. Not enough money or status, Tom had replied, channelling his mother. Juliet wondered what Veronica and Henry had thought of their son marrying a lowly librarian without a degree to her name.

"As did Simon," Veronica was saying. Simon was Tom's younger brother. "Of course, Dilly II went to Benenden before her medical training."

Juliet blinked. Another Dilly? How many women called Dilly were in the family? God forbid there should be a second Veronica.

"Yes, Sarah says Bedales suited her two down to the ground," said Tom. "Though I wouldn't want to send ours so far away."

When Tom raised his eyebrows questioningly at Juliet, she murmured agreement, sensing that if she tried to make a case for the local state school, he would not support her. She looked away.

Then it dawned on her. If Simon's wife was called Sarah, then Dilly must be a pet-name. But why the number? No, not a pet-name – an acronym, for convenience. Dilly – DIL – daughter-in-law. Suddenly, Juliet realised that all evening, Veronica hadn't once called her by name. To Veronica, she was just Dilly I – her daughter-in-law whose prime purpose and only value was to produce her precious grandchildren.

9 Anonymous

"I think that went well, darling, don't you?"

It was pitch dark as Henry reversed his car out of the drive and on to the lane, and Tom slid the bolt across the front door.

Juliet wasn't sure how to answer. The evening had been efficient and functional: meal eaten, drinks consumed, cigars smoked (by the men). But for her, it had been a shocking revelation. Despite Tom's professional status as a successful dentist, he was living in thrall to his much richer parents, dominated by his objectionable mother. Veronica had only spoken to Juliet to express disappointment, disagreement or disdain. Yet Tom seemed oblivious to her rudeness.

Lingering in the hall, Tom moved in on Juliet clumsily. As he put his arms about her, he misjudged the distance between them. His hand slipped off her shoulder and fell awkwardly at her side.

Juliet took a step back.

"Let's leave the washing up until the morning, shall we, darling? You can do it after I've gone to work." As he tried to draw her closer to him, she flinched at the blend of cigar smoke and stale red wine fumes drowning out his cologne. "Let's just get to bed."

When Tom stumbled and trod on her toe, Juliet realised he was drunker than she'd thought. She tried to remain calm.

"You go on upstairs while I put the casserole dish in to soak and load the dishwasher. I don't want to come down to a pile of dirty dishes in the morning. It'll only take me a minute."

Tom, needing no further persuasion, headed unsteadily for the stairs.

Earlier, Juliet had wondered why Tom had opened two bottles of red wine, ostensibly for his father, when it was clear that Henry would have to drive home at the end of the evening. Henry had only taken a small glass, and Veronica, after her fancy gin and tonic, had stuck to sparkling water – as had Juliet, wanting to keep her wits about her. Yet as she cleared the table, she discovered both wine bottles were empty.

She was unsure what to do. Tom must be very drunk indeed. Perhaps she shouldn't stay until the morning after all, but was she safe to drive? Although she'd drunk relatively little with the meal, what with the pre-dinner cocktails, she might still be over the legal limit. Even if she wasn't, Tom's Lexus was blocking her exit from the turning circle, and he was in no fit state to move it.

If she had already metabolised all the alcohol in her system, she would still be nervous negotiating those narrow, winding lanes alone in the dark. She didn't even know where she was exactly. She presumed the satnav would lead her back to Dave's Magic Motor Repairs, but there was no guarantee. Wasn't it better to stay put than end up somewhere even stranger?

No, she'd just have to make her escape after Tom had gone to work next day. In any case, Rob wasn't expecting her home till morning. She just hoped that when she left this madhouse, she would be able to return to her old life. It wasn't so bad, really, was it? She pictured Rob, most likely still down the pub, and wondered who was drunker, Rob or Tom.

Juliet turned on the dishwasher, crept to the foot of the stairs and listened for sounds from above. Tom's reverberating snores were the deep, steady kind fuelled by excess alcohol. She knew from her experience with Rob that Tom would be spark out till morning. She'd be safe enough sleeping beside him. She could just curl up at the edge of that big, comfortable bed.

As she climbed the stairs on tiptoe, she decided to allow herself one final taste of luxury. She lifted the crystal vase of lilacs carefully from her dressing table and moved it into the en suite bathroom, where she ran a deep bath with a generous glug of expensive designer bubble bath. As she sank beneath the foam, the steam brought out the intoxicating scent of rare spices.

She closed her eyes to think. Did she really want to return to Rob? Did he even exist for her to return to?

"That's me gone," he had said over the phone only hours before. Perhaps the safest bet would to drive to the nearest police station in the morning, report herself missing, then a few days later turn herself in and see who came forward to claim her.

She'd once read in a magazine that anyone could make an anonymous report of a missing person. You didn't even have to wait for the person to be missing for very long if you had cause to worry about them. The police would just ask for a list of their friends and relations, favourite places they might visit, photos and description. They'd also ask for DNA from a toothbrush or hairbrush. She could easily do all that, though she might have to disguise herself a little first, so that they didn't recognise her from her own description.

Within forty-eight hours, they'd pass the information to all other UK forces. If anyone else in the country – including Rob and Tom – was looking for Juliet, they would surely contact the police. That still didn't mean she had to go back to either of them. For a missing person over the age of eighteen, the police would not reveal their whereabouts to an enquirer without their permission.

Who do I want to claim me? she wondered. Rob or Tom, or – she gulped – neither of them?

Then she realised. It wasn't the police who would solve her problem. It was Dave. Dave's Magic Motor

Repairs. His little purple Mini had got her into this mess. Dave would have the answer when she returned the car to him in the morning. All she needed to do was set the satnav to "home".

As goosebumps dotted her naked flesh, she sank further beneath the hot foam.

10 Love

"Porridge, love?" Juliet called up the stairs.

A low groan was all that emerged from the bedroom until twenty minutes later, when slow heaving footsteps heralded the arrival of a sheepish Tom, dressed in a smart shirt and trousers ready for work. Juliet had already made his porridge and set it to keep warm in the Aga. Quite versatile, these Agas, she'd decided, after making herself some toast on the open hotplate, although too fussy and showy for anyone other than farmers who needed their warming cupboard to revive new-born lambs. They'd make the kitchen far too hot other than in winter. Even though it was still early in the day, the kitchen was unpleasantly close already. In the summer, it must be positively Saharan.

Even so, Juliet was feeling refreshed and revitalised. On waking an hour before, she had indulged in an energising shower beneath the rainfall setting of the elaborate head in the en suite, making extravagant use of the expensive gel and body lotions on the bathroom shelves. The cubicle alone was almost as big as her whole bathroom at home. After cleaning her teeth (fortunately, she'd found a new head for the electric toothbrush, so that she didn't have to use Tom's wife's), she ran her tongue over her newly-filled tooth. There was no filling. The tooth was still whole.

Returning to the bedroom where Tom slept on, she chose from the wardrobe a timeless sea-green floral tea dress. Paired with a soft, faded denim jacket and lavender suede pumps, it made the perfect outfit for a beautiful spring day. Juliet hoped the dress would still fit her once she'd left the house. She didn't want to do an Incredible Hulk act, bursting her buttons if her life-preserver returned in front of the mechanics at Dave's Magic Motor Repairs.

"Porridge," echoed Tom, as if trying to convince himself he had an appetite for it. Shoulders hunched, he sank on to a high stool at the breakfast bar.

Juliet beamed as she set in front of him a crystal tumbler of freshly squeezed orange juice, having earlier discovered that the squat shiny cylinder beside the coffee machine was an electric juicer.

"What a lovely healthy start to the day!" she declared, dropping a pod into the coffee maker.

She'd mastered that gadget the night before while making after-dinner coffee for herself and Veronica, while Tom helped himself and Henry to brandy. Henry had left his glass untouched, so Tom had downed it.

As Juliet pressed the on button, Tom flinched at the sound of the motor. Juliet suppressed a smile. He'd be in for a lot worse than that when he reached his surgery.

Leaving Tom eating in sullen silence, Juliet took her own coffee out on to the terrace to enjoy the view of the post-dawn glory of the garden. The lawn was still damp with dew, and the lilac blossom sparkled in the early morning sun.

She slipped off her suede pumps to avoid matting their nap on the wet grass and strolled down the terrace steps and across the lawn. The bench beneath the lilacs had already dried in the sunshine, so she sat down without a care and gazed back up at the vast, elegant house.

This could have been her domain, if only she'd let Tom walk her home that night after the school disco. It was far too big for a family of four, though. Too much to clean, to furnish, to maintain, even if she didn't have to go out to work. It was the sort of house that would enslave you. Big properties were not all they were cracked up to be, especially when still owned by several mortgage companies. No wonder he had to accept his parents' charity to pay the kids' school fees.

As for Tom, he was far more high maintenance than she'd expected. Gorgeous and charming when he wanted to be, but at what cost to herself? No job, no freedom, no say in what really mattered in her life. Remembering the lavish wedding photo in the study, she realised his parents had probably paid for all that, too.

Her own mother could not have afforded it. Veronica probably picked up the tab on condition that she could art-direct the wedding to impress her friends.

So Tom was not The One after all. Might she have been happier had she married any other old flames? Would any of them truly have been able to offer her the sort of life she craved?

A large ginger cat leapt down from the neighbour's wall and trotted over to join her.

"No," she said aloud to the cat. "Only I can do that."

"Meow," replied the cat, rubbing its cheek against her bare legs.

"How?" echoed Juliet. "I'm not sure, but I have a feeling I'm about to find out."

When she leaned back to think, the cat leapt up and settled on her lap. She was still stroking its soft back when Tom appeared on the terrace, jangling his car keys in his hand. He forced a smile, still not admitting to his hangover.

"That's me gone now, Gems," he called, blowing her a kiss.

Feeling sorry for him now, she kissed her hand to him.

"Goodbye, Tom" she said, more to the cat than anyone.

While he started the Lexus and reversed down the drive and into the lane, Juliet remained in the garden. Did he even own that fancy car, she wondered, or was it an expensive lease and another drain on his resources?

She glanced at her watch. Just gone eight. On a working day, by now she'd be on the bus to her job at the library. She was always happy to return to work after her days off; although it was a job without prospects.

But today, her priority was to return the Mini to Dave, ready for his next borrower. As she still didn't know exactly where Tom's house was, she was unsure how long it would take to get back to Cirencester, so she decided to set off straight away. She scooped the cat off her lap and set it down gently on all fours. Purring, it settled to wash its paws while she picked up her mug and walked back to the patio, pausing only to pick a sprig of lavender for her buttonhole.

In the kitchen, she helped herself to a vintage wicker shopping basket and dropped in an apple from the overloaded fruit bowl, a bottle of French sparkling water from the big fridge, her handbag and car key. Then she went to take a last look around the study.

In the light of last night's experience, the big wedding photo was even more gruesome than she'd remembered. Clearly uncomfortable in her expensive dress, she must have spent the whole reception in fear of spilling something down her front.

In the picture of Eleanor and Edward with Veronica and Henry, the children looked as if they were being photographed under duress. If Veronica could make Juliet squirm as a grown-up, how difficult she must make life for her poor grandchildren.

In the holiday photos of Tom and herself, their smiles looked forced and phoney. Perhaps neither of them had wanted to go to the destination dictated that year by Veronica.

Without more ado, Juliet turned her back on them all and headed for the front door. The Mini was gleaming beneath a spritz of dew. She unlocked the door, slid comfortably into the leather seat and set her basket down on the passenger side before fastening her seatbelt. As soon as she turned on the ignition, the satnav screen lit up and Juliet pressed the "home" button.

More rain overnight had refreshed the winding country lanes, and the hedgerows were gleaming and buoyant beneath the morning sun. At the first sound of the satnav's voice that had reminded her so much of Tom's, she switched to the female alternative. This voice sounded strong and intelligent, like the sort of person Juliet would choose as a friend. In fact, it was not unlike Maisie's.

Together, they proceeded at a leisurely pace, Juliet enjoying the satnav lady's insightful observations on the scenery and losing all track of time until they joined the Cirencester ring road from the Burford direction. At 10.59am precisely, the purple Mini glided neatly into the space reserved for the courtesy car at Dave's Magic Motor Repairs.

Still relaxed from her interesting and informative journey, Juliet smiled warmly at the mechanics as she stepped out of the car. She was pleased to notice they just smiled back and waved, rather than greeting her by her unwelcome nickname. One of the mechanics was singing along to a golden oldie playing on the radio, the first record she'd bought as a teenager all those years ago.

Juliet marched across the car park and tapped lightly on the door of Dave's office. Perching on Dave's stool was a man with his distinctive crinkly hair and beard, but now they were nut-brown. What hard work it must be to dye his hair when there was so much of it. Yet it was a flattering look, the colour making his complexion far less lined and his eyebrows less bushy. Dave looked as if he'd been professionally photoshopped.

He interrupted her thoughts. "Nice drive, love?"

Juliet hesitated, wondering how much he might know of what she'd just been through. She chose her words carefully.

"Beautiful scenery. Useful thinking time."

Dave nodded his approval.

"Yes, it's a good little car for a solo journey." He put his head on one side. "I'm surprised you decided to bring it back."

Juliet gave a wistful smile as she set the Mini's keys reverently on the counter. "I wish I didn't have to. It's much nicer than Rob's car."

She glanced at the pegboard on the wall, searching for Rob's distinctive key, but it wasn't there. Dave slapped his hand to his forehead.

"Sorry, love, I've just remembered. The replacement lamp for your car didn't come in with our delivery yesterday afternoon, so we've not had the chance to fix it yet. In fact, it may take a little while to come in as it's a non-standard part. Of course, it's illegal to drive as it is now, so I'm afraid you'll have to hang on to the Mini for a bit longer."

Juliet's face lit up. "That's fine by me. But what about the customer who's meant to have it from eleven today?"

Dave looked down at his appointments diary and jabbed a finger at the name against 11am.

"You're in luck, love. Just before you arrived, he phoned to cancel." He pulled a pen from the top pocket beneath his beard and struck a line through the name. "In fact, he's poorly, so he's not sure when he's going to be in now. So you can keep the Mini as long as you like."

"Oh well, if you're sure…"

"No trouble to me, love."

Before Dave could change his mind, Juliet scooped up the Mini's keys and clutched them to her chest. As she turned to go, Dave called after her, "Nice dress, by the way, love, if you don't mind me saying."

She glanced down at the tea dress, which flared elegantly from her slender waist.

"Thanks, Dave. I'll see you, er, whenever."

Dave smiled.

"Whenever is just fine."

As she left the office, her head began to fill with fond memories of the old purple Mini that had been her first car. She'd been sad to sell it to pay for her and Rob's honeymoon. No satnavs in those days, of course. She'd depended on her own navigational skills. She liked it better that way.

She blinked as she stepped out of the gloomy office and on to the bright forecourt. It must have been a trick of the morning light, so clear after the previous day's rain, but the courtesy car now looked a slightly different shape – exactly like the Mini she had driven in her teens.

11 Juliet

Comfortable behind the wheel, Juliet didn't even notice that the satnav had vanished from the dashboard. Not that she needed a satnav. She'd done this route so often, she could trust her internal auto-pilot.

Slowing down behind a tractor that was hesitating at a roundabout, Juliet checked in the rear-view mirror to see how many cars were queuing behind her. The reflected sunshine made her dark auburn hair glint like copper thread.

The tractor lurched into motion, and she drove on, taking her favourite scenic route, enjoying seeing the countryside morph from the soft, low hills of the Cotswolds through the leafy Forest of Dean into the more dramatic Brecon Beacons, the road rising, rising, and the sky growing bigger with every mile she travelled. Beyond the tourist attractions, where fencing fields became optional, she slowed down to avoid a chubby lamb trotting along the roadside towards its mother, alarmed at the Mini's engine noise. The bond between ewe and lamb always warmed her heart. Perhaps one day, she'd be a mother and feel such maternal instincts herself, but not for a long time yet.

Juliet had expected her own mother to object to her plan to go to such a distant university on leaving school, but she'd been only proud and encouraging. Juliet had saved up for the Mini so that she could drive home to see her mum as often as she liked during term-time. Her part-time job in the university library paid for its running costs plus petrol.

Soon bright bluebells dotted the verges, and Juliet wound down the window to catch their scent. She looked forward to strolling through the bluebell woods between the town and the campus later that day. It was her favourite route to and from lectures at this time of year.

Now great horse chestnut trees were towering over her, laden with candelabra-like blossoms in cream and pale pink. The treeline thinned as the road ascended beyond the Brecon Beacons to the high, bare terrain with a different kind of wild beauty that would characterise the rest of her journey. As usual, her ears popped as she summited the highest point and began to glide gently down the other side. The winding hillside road twisted towards an opalescent sea beyond matte slate rocks in a curvaceous double bay.

Croeso i Aberystwyth.

As Juliet followed the main road down to the sea front, only the knowledge that she had to be back at her flat by two o'clock made her resist the temptation to park beneath the old castle and go for a stroll along the promenade. She relished the familiar sea breeze in her hair and the tang of salt on her lips, but she was on a promise.

At the far end of the north bay, past the pier, she turned back inland and down a side street. There was just enough space to slip the Mini into its usual parking place between a turquoise Ford Capri and a yellow Hillman Imp. Grabbing her basket, she stepped out of the car on to the pavement.

Maisie was calling to her from the nearest doorway. Behind her, narrow stairs led up to their flat above the wool shop. They'd been lucky to nab this place as their third-year digs after spending the first year in halls and the second sharing a bigger house with two other girls and three boys.

"You're right on time," said Maisie, "but your friend Monty was early. He must be keen. I've made him a coffee and left him upstairs on the sofa reading his book, but I must dash now. I've got a lecture at half past."

Juliet hastened to the foot of the stairs before Maisie could broadcast any more of her business to the street.

"Thanks, Maisie, I owe you."

Maisie shrugged. "He looks like the type who'd wait for you all day. He's spent the last ten minutes telling me how wonderful you are."

"No wonder you're so keen to rush off to your lecture."

Maisie laughed. "Well, I'd hate to play gooseberry."

Juliet didn't want to keep him waiting any longer. She had promised to give him her decision today. She ran up the stairs two at a time.

When she opened the door that led from the tiny square landing into their small sitting room, a young blond man with kind grey eyes and a wide mouth looked up from his battered paperback. Montague was a History student whom she'd befriended in the university library. Lately, he'd been trying to persuade her to apply for the postgraduate degree in Librarianship that he was planning to do the following year. The most welcome chat-up line she'd ever had, she'd told Maisie.

As Juliet set her basket down on the ancient but pristine coffee table, he stuck his student union card in his book to mark his place and stuffed it in his denim satchel. His generous mouth broadened into the warmest of smiles.

"Hello, Juliet," he said. "It's lovely to see you. Sorry to be here before you were, I was just so eager to know your decision. I mean, I don't want to rush you or put pressure on you, but you know tomorrow is the closing date for the MSc course? I've already put in my application."

When Juliet stepped around the table to sit beside him on the sofa, he budged up to allow her more space.

"I really hope you want to do it," he continued, "and not only so that we can spend another year at university together. The extra qualification would be the passport to a terrific career for you. You see –"

Gently Juliet laid a hand on his arm.

"It's OK, Montague, no further persuasion needed. I put my application in weeks ago, before I even met you. My tutor told me I'm bound to be offered a place. I'm so glad, because I've known for years that I want to be a career librarian."

"So do you think you'll accept the place?"

His earnest eyes met hers, and she smiled.

"I do."

THANK YOU FOR READING
MRS MORRIS CHANGES LANES

Book reviews help authors sell more books.
If you enjoyed reading this book,
please consider posting
a brief review online.
Word-of-mouth recommendations
will also be much appreciated.
Thank you.

FOR A FREE EBOOK

Join Debbie Young's Readers' Club
at her website
www.authordebbieyoung.com
and you will be sent a link
to claim your free copy of
The Pride of Peacocks,
an entertaining novelette
set in the Cotswolds.

Also by Debbie Young

Sophie Sayers Village Mysteries *(Novels)*

Best Murder in Show
Trick or Murder?
Murder in the Manger
Murder by the Book
Springtime for Murder
Murder Your Darlings
Murder Lost and Found

St Bride's School Stories for Grown-ups *(Novels)*

Secrets at St Bride's
Stranger at St Bride's

Tales from Wendlebury Barrow *(Novellas)*

The Natter of Knitters
The Clutch of Eggs

Short Story Collections

Marry in Haste – 15 Stories of Dating, Love and Marriage
Quick Change – Tiny Tales of Transformation
Stocking Fillers – 12 Short Stories for Christmas

Essay Collections

All Part of the Charm – A Memoir of Modern Village Life
Still Charmed
Young By Name – Whimsical Columns from the Tetbury Advertiser
Still Young By Name

Acknowledgments

As ever, huge thanks to my terrific publishing team: my editor, Alison Jack, proofreader Dan Gooding and designer Rachel Lawston, who produced the most wonderful original drawing as part of her design for the cover, and to my beta readers Lucienne Boyce and Amie McCracken, for saving me from myself.

The notion of a satnav controlled by a real person in a remote tower was the brainchild of my daughter Laura when she was younger, so she deserves the credit for the germ of the satnav storyline.

I'd like to thank the NHS for its excellent dental service, and in particular the dentists whose upbeat chairside manner inspired the storyline.

The beautiful beard of the proprietor of Dave's Magic Motor Repairs was inspired by that of retired bookseller and all-round legend Peter Snell, the much-loved former proprietor of Barton's Bookshop, Leatherhead.

With thanks to the late Christopher Isherwood for suggesting the title of my novella with his wonderful novel, *Mr Norris Changes Trains*, entirely different from my book in every other respect.

Debbie Young

Printed in Great Britain
by Amazon